E
MA

Mayer, Mercer

A boy, a dog, and a
frog

$8.89

A BOY, A DOG and A FROG

by Mercer Mayer

DIAL BOOKS FOR YOUNG READERS
New York

To my family,
Marianna and Samantha

Published by Dial Books for Young Readers
A division of E. P. Dutton | A division of New American Library
2 Park Avenue, New York, New York 10016
Copyright © 1967 by Mercer Mayer. All rights reserved.
Library of Congress Catalog Card Number: 67-22254
Printed in Hong Kong by South China Printing Co.
C O B E
14 16 18 20 19 17 15 13